· Gordon ·

· Harold ·

· Percy ·

THOMAS
THE TANK ENGINE
& FRIENDS

Based on
The Railway Series
by The Rev W Awdry

Thomas and Trevor
by Christopher Awdry
based on original material
by Britt Allcroft and David Mitton
and *Duck Takes Charge*

Ladybird Books

Acknowledgment
*Photographic stills by David Mitton and Terry Permane
for Britt Allcroft (Thomas) Ltd.*

British Library Cataloguing in Publication Data

Awdry, W.
    Thomas and Trevor; Duck takes charge.—
    (Thomas the Tank Engine & Friends; 9)
    I. Title   II. Awdry, Christopher
    III. Awdry, W. Thomas and Trevor   IV. Series
    823′.914[J]   PZ7
    ISBN 0-7214-1006-5

Thomas and Trevor

Thomas and Trevor

Trevor the Traction Engine enjoys living in the vicarage orchard on the Island of Sodor. Edward the Blue Engine once helped to save him from being turned into scrap so now Trevor lives at the vicarage and the two engines are great friends.

Edward comes to see Trevor every day. Sometimes Trevor is sad because he doesn't have enough work to do.

"I do like to keep busy all the time," Trevor sighed one day, "and I do like company, especially children's company."

"Cheer up," smiled Edward. "The Fat Controller has work for you at his new harbour – I'm to take you to meet Thomas today."

"Oh!" exclaimed Trevor happily. "A harbour, the seaside, children, that will be lovely."

Trevor's truck was coupled behind Edward and they set off to meet Thomas.

Thomas was on his way to the harbour with a trainload of metal pilings. They were needed to make the harbour wall firm and safe.

"Hello, Thomas," said Edward. "This is Trevor, a friend of mine. He's a Traction Engine."

Thomas eyed the newcomer doubtfully. "A *what* engine?" he asked.

"A Traction Engine," explained Trevor. "I run on roads instead of rails. Can you take me to the harbour, please? The Fat Controller has a job for me."

"Yes – of course," replied Thomas. But he was still puzzled.

Workmen coupled Trevor's truck to Thomas's train and soon they were ready to start their journey.

"I'm glad the Fat Controller needs me," called Trevor. "I don't have enough to do sometimes, you know, although I can work anywhere – in orchards, on farms, in scrapyards, even at harbours."

"But you don't run on rails," puffed Thomas.

"I'm a Traction Engine – I don't need rails to be useful," replied Trevor. "You wait and see."

When they reached the harbour they found everything in confusion. Trucks had been derailed, blocking the line, and stone slabs lay everywhere.

"We must get these pilings through," said Thomas's driver. "They are essential. Trevor," he said, "we need you to drag them round this mess."

"Just the sort of job I like," replied Trevor. "Now you'll see, Thomas – I'll soon show you what Traction Engines can do."

Trevor was as good as his word. First he dragged the stones clear with chains. Then he towed the pilings into position.

"Who needs rails?" he muttered cheerfully to himself.

Later Thomas brought his two coaches, Annie and Clarabel, to visit Trevor.

Thomas was most impressed. "Now I understand how useful a traction engine can be," he said.

Thomas's coaches were full of children and Trevor gave them rides along the harbour. Of all the jobs he did at the harbour that day, he liked this best of all.

"He's very kind," said Annie.

"He reminds me of Thomas," added Clarabel.

Everyone was sorry when it was time for Trevor to go. Thomas pulled him to the junction.

A small tear came into Trevor's eye. Thomas pretended not to see and whistled gaily to make Trevor happy.

"I'll come and see you if I can," Thomas promised. "The Vicar will look after you and there's plenty of work for you now at the orchard, but we may need you again at the harbour some day."

"That would be wonderful," said Trevor happily.

That evening, Trevor stood in the orchard remembering his new friend, Thomas, the harbour and most of all – the children. Then he went happily to sleep in the shed at the bottom of the orchard.

Duck takes charge

Duck takes charge

"Do you know what?" asked Percy.

"What?" grunted Gordon.

"Do you know what?"

"Silly," said Gordon, crossly, "of course I don't know what, if you don't tell me what what is."

"The Fat Controller says that the work in the yard is too heavy for me," said Percy. "He's getting a bigger engine to help me."

"Rubbish!" said James. "Any engine could do it," he went on grandly. "If you worked more and chattered less, this yard would be a sweeter, a better, and a happier place."

Percy went off to fetch some coaches.

"That stupid old signal," he thought. He was remembering the time when he had misunderstood a signal and gone backwards instead of forwards.

"No one listens to me now. They think I'm a silly little engine, and order me about. I'll show them! I'll show them!" he puffed as he ran about the yard. But he didn't know how. By the end of the afternoon he felt tired and unhappy.

He brought some of the coaches to the station and stood puffing at the side of the platform.

"Hello, Percy!" said the Fat Controller. "You look tired."

"Yes, sir, I am, sir," said Percy. "I don't know if I'm standing on my dome or my wheels."

"You look the right way up to me," laughed the Fat Controller. "Cheer up! The new engine is bigger than you, and can probably do the work alone. Would you like to help to build my new harbour? Thomas and Toby are helping."

"Oh yes, sir. Thank you, sir," said Percy happily.

The new engine arrived next morning.

"What's your name?" asked the Fat Controller kindly.

"Montague, sir. But I'm usually called 'Duck'," he replied. "They say I waddle."

The engine smiled. "I don't really, sir, but I like 'Duck' better than Montague."

"Good!" said the Fat Controller. "Duck it shall be. Here Percy, show Duck round."

The two engines went off together. Soon they were very busy.

James, Gordon and Henry watched Duck quietly doing his work.

"He seems a simple sort of engine," they whispered. "We'll have some fun and order him about."

"Quaa-aa-aak! Quaa-aa-aak!" they wheezed as they passed him.

Smoke billowed everywhere. Percy was cross, but Duck took no notice.

"They'll get tired of it soon," he said.
"Do they tell you to do things, Percy?"

"Yes they do!" answered Percy, crossly.

"Right," said Duck, "we'll soon stop *that* nonsense."

He whispered something to Percy and then said, "We'll do it later."

The Fat Controller had had a good day. He was looking forward to hot buttered toast for tea at home.

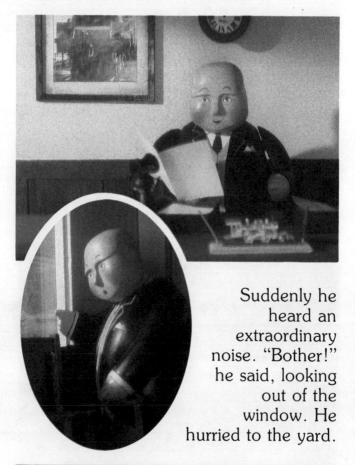

Suddenly he heard an extraordinary noise. "Bother!" he said, looking out of the window. He hurried to the yard.

Henry, Gordon and James were "wheeshing" and snorting furiously while Duck and Percy sat calmly on the points outside the shed, refusing to let the other engines in.

"STOP THAT NOISE," bellowed the Fat Controller.

"They won't let us in," hissed the big engines.

"Duck! Explain this behaviour," demanded the Fat Controller.

"Beg pardon, sir, but I'm a Great Western Engine. We do our work without fuss. But begging your pardon, sir, Percy and I would be glad if you would inform these – er – engines that we only take orders from you."

The big engines blew their whistles loudly.

"SILENCE!" snapped the Fat Controller.

"Percy and Duck," he said. "I am pleased with your work today; but *not* with your behaviour tonight. You have caused a disturbance."

Percy and Duck looked very worried.

Gordon, Henry and James sniggered.

"As for you," thundered the Fat Controller, "you've been worse. You made the disturbance! Duck is quite right. This is my railway and I give the orders."

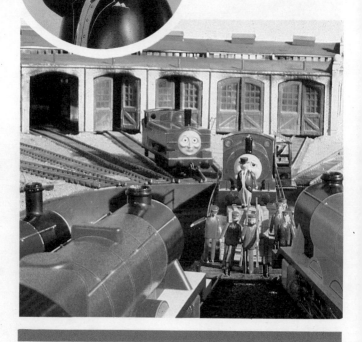

Later Percy went away and Duck was left to manage alone. And he did so... easily!

· Duck ·

· Diesel ·

· Daisy ·